GRANDMOTHER

Have the Angels Come?

by Denise Vega

illustrated by Erin Eitter Kono

LB
1837

E, BROWN AND COMPANY
Books for Young Readers
New York   Boston

Hachette Book Group USA

237 Park Avenue, New York, NY 10017

First Edition: February 2009

Little, Brown and Company

Visit our Web site at www.lb-kids.com

ISBN-13: 978-0-316-10663-4

ISBN-10: 0-316-10663-1

10 9 8 7 6 5 4 3 2 1

SC

Printed in China

The text was set in Mercurius and Pacella and the display type was hand-lettered by Maria Mercado

The illustrations for this book were done in acrylic and pencil on watercolor paper.

Book design by Maria Mercado

In memory of my maternal grandmother,
Inez Azcuenaga Wilcomb — D.V.

For Caitlyn Akiko, her Grandmamas, and mine — E.E.K.

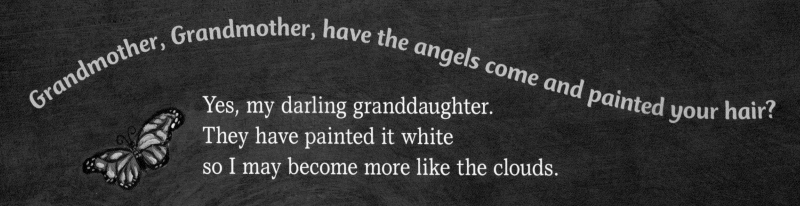

Grandmother, Grandmother, have the angels come and painted your hair?

Yes, my darling granddaughter.
They have painted it white
so I may become more like the clouds.

Will you float across blue skies
and make shapes for me to see?

Yes, my darling granddaughter.
I will float like cotton
and sprinkle rain upon your hair.

Grandmother, Grandmother, have the angels come and darkened your eyes?

Yes, my darling granddaughter.
They have dimmed my vision
so I may see more clearly.

Will you see me across mountains
and faraway places?

Yes, my darling granddaughter.
I will see you over valleys
and deep inside your soul.

Grandmother, Grandmother, have the angels come and covered your ears?

Yes, my darling granddaughter.
They have quieted the sounds
so I may hear even the sigh of a butterfly.

Will you hear me when it's loud and when it's silent?

Yes, my darling granddaughter.
I will hear the songs in your heart
and the Voice inside my own.

Grandmother, Grandmother, have the angels come
and taken your teeth?

Yes, my darling granddaughter.
They have plucked my teeth
so I may savor flavors long on my tongue.

Will you taste the wild honey
and drink my lemonade?

Yes, my darling granddaughter.
I will taste the sweetness of your Spirit
and we will drink the lasting waters.

Grandmother, Grandmother, have the angels come
and curved your back?

Yes, my darling granddaughter.
They have curved my back
so I may touch your face more easily.

Will I feel your touch when I'm awake
and when I sleep?

Yes, my darling granddaughter.
I will stroke your cheeks
in the light and in the darkness.

Grandmother, Grandmother, have the angels come
and bent your fingers?

Yes, my darling granddaughter.
They have bent my fingers
so I may hold your hand more tightly.

Will you hold me when I'm scared
and feeling all alone?

Yes, my darling granddaughter.
I will hold you when you fly
and when you fall.

Grandmother, Grandmother, have the angels come
and slowed your legs?

Yes, my darling granddaughter.
They have slowed my legs
so I may pause to see your beauty
reflected in the dewdrop on a flower.

Will we walk together across the meadows
and feel the breeze around our feet?

Yes, my darling granddaughter.
We will dance the slow dance of the sunset
reaching golden-pink fingers across the sky.

Grandmother, Grandmother, have the angels come
and curved your feet?

Yes, my darling granddaughter.
They have curved my feet
so I may perch beside you.

Will you sing me the songs of the earth
and the grasses?

Yes, my darling granddaughter.
I will sing of our laughter and our tears.

Grandmother, Grandmother, have the angels come?

Yes, my darling granddaughter, the angels have come.
They have painted my hair and darkened my eyes.
They have covered my ears and taken my teeth.
They have curved my back and bent my fingers.
They have slowed my legs and curved my feet.

And they have lit my heart with the fire of Love.

What will you do with this fire of Love?

I will touch my heart to your heart,
my light to your light.

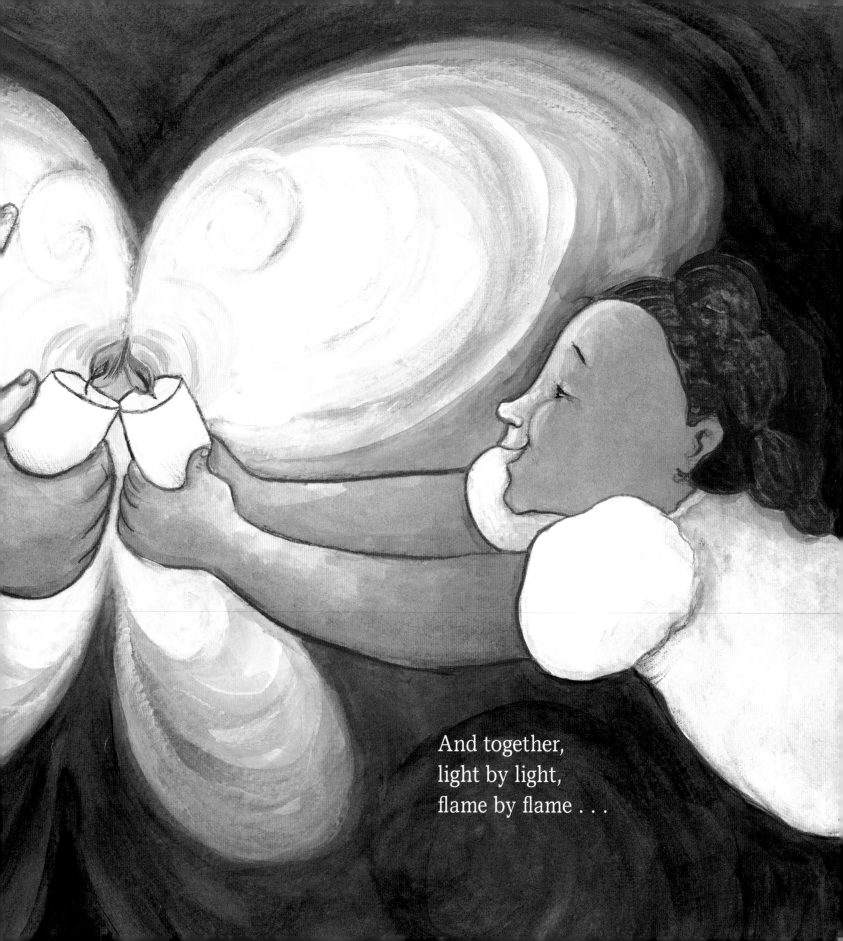

And together,
light by light,
flame by flame . . .

We will set the world on fire.